To my Larry - who always finds light in the dark.

RDX Collective
244 5th Avenue
New York, NY 10001

First Edition: September 2023

The text is set in Concourse.
The illustrations were drawn and painted digitally.

ISBN 979-8-9869953-3-5 (hardcover)
ISBN 979-8-9869953-2-8 (paperback)
ISBN 979-8-9869953-0-4 (eBook)
Library of Congress Control Number: 2023914735

Visit author's website www.raneetaylor.com
Learn more at www.mypatchworkfriends.com

Ranee Taylor

The Nightlight

illustrated by
Evgenia Malina

Patchworks have unique patterns and are stitched together with love.
They have odds and ends.

They have bits and pieces.
Patchworks are combinations of the animals before them.

Larry is a Patchwork Bear.
He is very courageous and very loyal.
He loves eating. He loves swimming.
He loves playing.
He is also afraid of the dark.

One day, he heard his family planning a camping trip.
Larry loved being outdoors but was scared of not sleeping in his room.
He asked his parents if he had to go.

Larry's mom said, "This is a family reunion.
All of the Patchwork Bears will be there."

Larry's dad said, "We will spend the day fishing and having fun."
His mom insisted, "I know you will love everything about camping."

The very next day, Larry's grandpa came to visit.

Larry's grandpa knew how to build anything and fix everything. Grandpa also made him feel very safe. Grandpa made the nightlight that comforted Larry when he went to sleep in his room.

Grandpa quickly saw how sad Larry was.
Larry told him that he was afraid of going camping.
He was scared of how dark everything would be at night.
Grandpa was very patient and listened to Larry talk.

Larry explained to Grandpa that he couldn't see anything in his room when it was dark. That he is afraid of what might be in the corner or under his bed.

Grandpa replied, "You can be big and brave and also afraid of the dark."

Grandpa said, "I also understand that it doesn't feel very good to be afraid." Grandpa reminded Larry that he has a very wonderful imagination. His imagination is what allows him to draw and to tell stories.

Grandpa told Larry to be proud of his imagination, even if it plays tricks on him at night.

That night Grandpa came to tuck Larry into bed.
Grandpa turned on the special nightlight and asked Larry

Grandpa put his hands close to the nightlight.

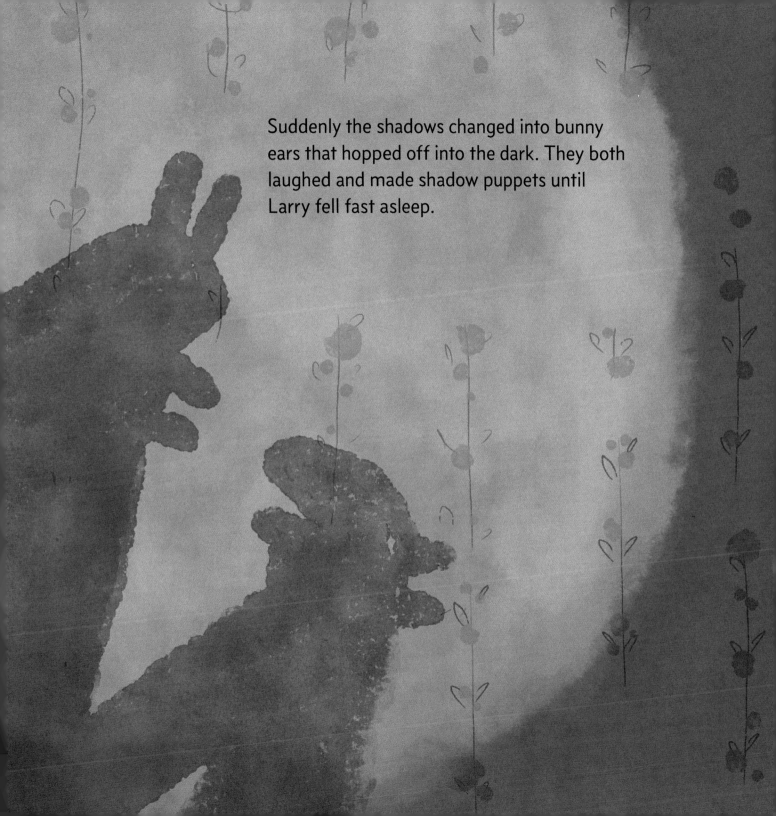

Suddenly the shadows changed into bunny ears that hopped off into the dark. They both laughed and made shadow puppets until Larry fell fast asleep.

In the morning, all of the Patchwork Bears
traveled to their very favorite camping spot.
They spent time eating.
They spent time swimming.
They spent time playing.

They were all very tired as the sun started
going down.

Larry snuggled close to his mom as the sky got darker.
The clouds changed from orange to red to purple.

A large campfire was started, and all of the Patchwork Bears gathered around. In the shadows, Larry saw all of the faces he loved the most.

As the sky went black, all the stars started to wake up and twinkle.
Grandpa pointed out constellations in the stars and told stories.

In the meadow across the way, Larry spotted tiny
slivers of light floating in the air.
Grandpa and Larry walked over to take a closer look.

Flying here and there were thousands of fireflies!
They disappeared and reappeared like magic in the dark.
They were glowing, very green and very yellow.

Grandpa had a small glass jar with a lid that he had poked a few holes in. As Grandpa removed the lid, one of the fireflies flew down into the jar.

Grandpa screwed on the lid and the entire jar glowed with that beautiful light. Grandpa told Larry that this could be his nightlight to go to sleep.

Larry thought the light was very nice.

But his imagination was now telling him how much fun he could have in the dark.

Larry told Grandpa that he wanted the firefly
to keep playing with his family.

Grandpa smiled and unscrewed the lid from
the jar. The firefly blinked three times and
flew off into the night.

Larry realized he was very sleepy as they walked back to camp.

Grandpa held Larry's hand and said he was very proud of him for facing his fear.

Larry then laid down, snuggled into his sleeping bag, and fell fast asleep.

Made in the USA
Middletown, DE
26 September 2023

39108424R00022